A dog called
ROD

tim hopgood

MACMILLAN CHILDREN'S BOOKS

My name is Elsa.

I live with my Dad on the very
top floor of a big block of flats.

From our kitchen window you can see right across the city.

I like to watch the people in the park walk their dogs. (From up here they look like tiny ants!)

I'd really like a pet.
If I could have a pet,
I'd choose a dog.

And if I had a dog, I'd call him Rod.

Dad says, **"The fun of having a pet to look after soon wears off."**

But I'm 100% sure that it wouldn't with me.

I'd teach Rod to play the keyboard and we'd sing songs together.

I've already painted lots of pictures of Rod
and stuck them on my bedroom wall.
Rod likes painting too! He likes modern art.

I've put Rod's paintings up inside my wardrobe.

That's his quiet place.

Dad says, **"Dogs make too much mess."**

But Dad doesn't know Rod!

Rod's so neat and tidy you wouldn't even know he was there. He always flushes the toilet and never leaves the seat up (like Dad!).

Dad says,
**"Dogs need
plenty of
exercise.
They like
lots of long
walks."**

Rod isn't that kind of dog.
He's not keen on long walks, he prefers to go by bike.

Dad says, "Dogs are very, **very noisy!**"

WOOF WOOF WOOF WOOF

WOOF!
WOOF!

woof woof

woof

Rod isn't.

Rod likes reading and sticking things in
my scrapbook, and quiet things like that.

There's always a reason why we can't have a dog.

"Vets' bills!" Dad says. **"A dog could cost a small fortune."**

But Rod's never ill.

He eats broccoli.
(And spaghetti bolognaise,
which is my favourite too!)

Then one morning
I get a big surprise . . .

Dad suddenly says,
**"Elsa, if you're
absolutely sure that
you want a dog, then
I'll think about it."**

"Hooray!" I say.

**"But on one
condition,"**
says Dad.

**"First of all
you must
look after
Barker for
a week."**

Barker belongs to Dad's friend Rita who lives on the ground floor.

Barker isn't like Rod.

He doesn't like singing or playing the piano and he barks when we are trying to read.

WOOF!
WOOF!
WOOF!

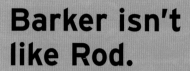

He always makes a mess when we paint and he leaves pawprints all over the place.

Barker doesn't like broccoli, he eats stinky dog food.

And he doesn't even ride a bike. He needs walking morning, noon and night.

Looking after Barker is really hard work.

I'm glad when Barker goes home.

"I think I'd like
a cat instead,"
I tell Rod.

But Rod says he thinks he might be allergic
to cats. They make his eyes itchy! Rod says
if he could have a pet, he'd really like a mouse.

I say, "Hmmm, I'll think about it."

In the morning, I tell Dad that instead of a dog I absolutely 100% postively want a mouse.

"A mouse?"
says Dad.
"Why a mouse?"

So I say,

"**A** mouse would be **perfect** because they don't **bark** at

night, they don't need **long walks**, you won't have to pick up

their **poo** in the park, they won't leave **muddy** pawprints

all over the place, they don't mind living **high up** on the very

top floor, they don't need lots of **grooming**, they don't eat

steak or anything **expensive** like that, and because they're

small the **vets' bills** will be too."

"Hmmm," says Dad.
"I'll think about it."

"**And** most importantly," I say.

"Rod wants a **mouse** too."

"**Well, in that case,**" says Dad.
"**Let's get one . . .**

"but who on earth is **Rod?**"

First published 2007 by Macmillan Children's Books
a division of Macmillan Publishers Limited
20 New Wharf Road, London N1 9RR
Basingstoke and Oxford
Associated companies throughout the world
www.panmacmillan.com

ISBN: 978-1-4050-9269-2

A CIP catalogue record for this book is available from the British Library.

Printed in China